THE GREEN-FINGERED WITCH

For Isla, Leo and Molly,
and for Stephen, my green-fingered stepdad

H. D.

For the magical River Espinosa Chatterton

S. L.

First published in paperback in the United Kingdom by HarperCollins *Children's Books* in 2024

HarperCollins *Children's Books* is a division of HarperCollins*Publishers* Ltd
1 London Bridge Street, London SE1 9GF

www.harpercollins.co.uk

HarperCollins*Publishers*
Macken House, 39/40 Mayor Street Upper, Dublin 1, D01 C9W8, Ireland

1 3 5 7 9 10 8 6 4 2

This book contains FSC™ certified paper and other controlled
sources to ensure responsible forest management.

For more information visit: www.harpercollins.co.uk/green

THE GREEN-FINGERED WITCH

Helen Docherty

Illustrated by Steven Lenton

HARPERCOLLINS
CHILDREN'S BOOKS

On the first night at Witch School, at quarter to eight,
the new class was ready – but one witch was late.
She tried to squeeze on to the end of the line.
Ms Birch shook her head; this was not a good sign.

This last witch looked **strange**. Something wasn't quite right:
dungarees, wellies – and no hat in sight.
Even her hair was suspiciously clean!
Only one thing was **witchlike**: her fingers were green.

"Why aren't you wearing the proper witch dress?
What's your name, anyway?"

"Please, miss, I'm Cress."

Broomsticks were given to each witch in turn.
Ms Birch said, "You should find this easy to learn."

While the other young witches went zooming around,
poor Cress found it tricky to get off the ground.
"Come on, broomstick!" she whispered. Her broom gave a quiver.
It leaped in the air . . .

. . . and threw Cress in the river.

The next lesson was spells. The witches prepared.
"We'll start with an easy one," Ms Birch declared.
"Take these ingredients; mix them up well.
Read out these words and you should have your spell."

The others had finished before very long,
but Cress knew her spell had gone horribly wrong.
Her potion was bubbling, faster and faster.
She could see this was destined to end in disaster . . .

The results of her spell were quite hard to ignore;
they covered the ceiling, the walls and the floor.
Which witch had made such a terrible mess?
Ms Birch knew already: it had to be Cress!

Cress was embarrassed.
She felt such a fool.
Maybe she didn't
belong at this school?

By the time Cress got home, she was starting to yawn.
The sun had just risen; a beautiful dawn.
Most witches would sleep in the daytime, she knew;
but Cress had a hundred and one things to do . . .

. . . like planting her cabbages,
peas and broad beans,

onions and garlic
and tasty spring greens;

harvesting apples
and all kinds of squash;
pumpkins; potatoes
(in need of a wash).

And while her green fingers
worked quickly, Cress sighed.
She'd never learn magic,
as hard as she tried.

Back at school, all her efforts continued to fail.

Her flying was hopeless. Her potions were pale.

When her friends turned invisible . . .

Cress was still there.

Why couldn't she do it? It didn't seem fair.

Halloween was approaching: a night full of thrills,
and a chance for the witches to show off their skills.
Only Cress was unhappy. Her spirits were low.
She couldn't do magic; she'd nothing to show.

Then, late in October, Ms Birch lost her voice.
Lessons were cancelled – she'd no other choice.
Worse still, all the pumpkins that should have arrived
had dropped off a lorry . . . Not one had survived!

NO
SCHOOL
NO
PUMPKINS!

"Ms Birch, can you magic some pumpkins instead?"

But No Voice meant No Spells, and Ms Birch shook her head.

Halloween without pumpkins? It just couldn't be!

"I can help," offered Cress . . .

" . . . if you all follow me . . . "

Her friends were amazed to see what she'd grown.

"Did you do this yourself, Cress?"

"All on your own?"

They took one pumpkin each (Cress had plenty to spare).
Then they carried them back to the school, with great care.

The witches worked hard.
They each chose a group:

some carved
the pumpkins,

while others made soup.

As Ms Birch sipped the soup, her lost voice returned.
"You each have a talent – that's one thing I've learned.
Cress, you're a star; you have saved Halloween.
It's lucky that somebody's fingers are green!"

And now, Cress is happy; for everyone knows
that her magic lives in the things that she grows.